Something Else

For Carys – K.C.

Something Else

KATHRYN CAVE

Illustrated by **CHRIS RIDDELL**

PUFFIN

On a windy hill
alone
with nothing to be friends with
lived Something Else.

He knew that was what he was because everyone said so.

If he tried to sit with them
or walk with them
or join in their games,
they always said:

"Sorry. You're not like us.
You're something else.
You don't belong."

Something Else did his best
to be like the others.

He smiled and said "Hi!" like they did.

He painted pictures.

He played their games when they let him.

He brought his lunch in a paper bag like theirs.

It was no good.

He didn't look like them
or talk like them.

He didn't see the things they saw.

He didn't play the way they played.

As for his
packed lunches...

"You don't belong here," they said.
"You're not like us. You're something else."

Something Else went home.
While he was getting ready for bed,
there was a knock on the door.

Something was standing on the doorstep.
"Hi there!" it said. "Great to meet you. Can I come in?"
"Excuse me?" said Something Else.

"You're welcome," said the creature.
It stuck out a paw, or maybe a flipper.

Something Else looked at the paw.
"I think you've come to the wrong place," he said.

The creature shook its head. "No, I haven't.
This place is perfect. Look!"

And before Something Else realized what was happening,
it walked right in...

...and sat down on his supper.

"Do I know you?" asked Something Else, puzzled.

"Know me?" The creature laughed. "Of course you do!

Take a good look. Go on!"

Something Else looked.

He walked round the creature from front to back or back to front. He didn't know what to say, so he didn't say anything.

"Don't you see?" the creature cried. "I'm just like you! You're something else, and I'M ONE TOO!" It stuck out its paw again and smiled.

Something Else was too surprised to smile back.
He didn't take the paw either.

"Like me?" he said. "You're not like me.
In fact, you're not like anything I've ever seen.
I'm sorry, but you're definitely not MY sort of something else."
He walked to the door and opened it. "Goodnight."

The creature put down its paw, slowly.
"Oh," it said.
It looked sadder and smaller.

It reminded Something Else of something,
but he couldn't think what.

While he was trying to remember, the creature left.

Then Something Else remembered.
"Wait!" he cried. "Don't go!"

He ran after the creature as fast as he could.

When he caught up, he grabbed its paw and held on tight.

"You're not like me, BUT I DON'T MIND.

You can stay with me if you'd like to."

And the creature did.

From then on, Something Else had Something to be friends with.

They smiled and said "Hi!" to each other.

They painted pictures.

They played each other's games, or tried to.

They ate their lunches side by side.

They were different,
but they got along.

And when something turned up that really WAS weird-looking, they didn't say he wasn't like them and he didn't belong there.

They moved right up
and made room for him too.

PUFFIN BOOKS
Published by the Penguin Group: London, New York, Australia,
Canada, India, Ireland, New Zealand and South Africa
Penguin Books Ltd, Registered Offices: 80 Strand, London WC2R 0RL, England

puffinbooks.com

First published by Viking 1994
Published in Puffin Books 1995
Published in this edition 2011
001 – 10 9 8 7 6 5 4 3 2 1
Text copyright © Kathryn Cave, 1994
Illustrations copyright © Chris Riddell, 1994
All rights reserved
The moral right of the author and illustrator has been asserted
Made and printed in China
ISBN: 978–0–141–33867–5